BONES
and the DOG GONE Mystery

A Puffin Easy-to-Read

BY DAVID A. ADLER

ILLUSTRATED BY BARBARA JOHANSEN NEWMAN

PUFFIN BOOKS

For my great-nephews, Yagel Yaacov and Naftali Yair. —D. A.

For my son, Mike: You are sweet to the core. —B. J. N.

PUFFIN BOOKS
Published by the Penguin Group
Penguin Young Readers Group, 345 Hudson Street, New York, New York 10014, U.S.A.
Penguin Group (Canada), 90 Eglinton Avenue East, Suite 700, Toronto, Ontario, Canada M4P 2Y3
(a division of Pearson Penguin Canada Inc.)
Penguin Books Ltd, 80 Strand, London WC2R 0RL, England
Penguin Ireland, 25 St Stephen's Green, Dublin 2, Ireland (a division of Penguin Books Ltd)
Penguin Group (Australia), 250 Camberwell Road, Camberwell, Victoria 3124, Australia
(a division of Pearson Australia Group Pty Ltd)
Penguin Books India Pvt Ltd, 11 Community Centre,
Panchsheel Park, New Delhi - 110 017, India
Penguin Group (NZ), 67 Apollo Drive, Rosedale, North Shore 0632, New Zealand
(a division of Pearson New Zealand Ltd)
Penguin Books (South Africa) (Pty) Ltd, 24 Sturdee Avenue,
Rosebank, Johannesburg 2196, South Africa

Registered Offices: Penguin Books Ltd, 80 Strand, London WC2R 0RL, England

First published in the United States of America by Viking,
a division of Penguin Young Readers Group, 2004
Published by Puffin Books, a division of Penguin Young Readers Group, 2008

4 5 6 7 8 9 10

Text copyright © David A. Adler, 2004
Illustrations copyright © Barbara Johansen Newman, 2004
All rights reserved

THE LIBRARY OF CONGRESS HAS CATALOGED THE VIKING EDITION AS FOLLOWS:
Adler, David A.
Bones and the dog gone mystery / by David A. Adler ;
illustrated by Barbara Johansen Newman.
p.   cm.—(A Viking easy-to-read) (Bones ; 2)
Summary: While looking for his lost magnifying glass in the park, young
Detective Jeffrey Bones and his grandfather discover that Curly the detective dog
is missing, too, and start tracking down clues.
ISBN: 0-670-05948-X (hardcover)
[1. Lost and found possessions—Fiction. 2. Magnifying glasses—Fiction.
3. Dogs—Fiction. 4. Mystery and detective stories.]
I. Newman, Barbara Johansen, ill. II. Title. III. Series.
PZ7.A2615Bop 2004 [fic]—dc22 2004000827

Puffin Books ISBN 978-0-14-241043-1
Puffin® and Easy-to-Read® are registered trademarks of Penguin Group (USA) Inc.
Manufactured in China
Set in Bookman

- CONTENTS -

1. I'm Bones

I'm Bones,

Jeffrey Bones.

I'm a famous detective.

I find clues.

I solve mysteries.

One morning Grandpa gave me
a new magnifying glass.
It was bigger than my old one.
I held it up and looked
at my detective bag.
Wow!
That's a big bag.

I took my old magnifying glass

out of the bag and looked at it.

Hey!

Through my big new glass,

my small old glass looked bigger

than my big new glass.

What?

That was too confusing.

"Let's go," Grandpa said.

"Let's take Curly to the park."

Curly is Grandpa's dog.

He's a detective dog.

I've tried to fool Curly.

I've put on lots of disguises,

but Curly always knew it was me.

Curly pulled on his leash.

Grandpa and I had to hurry to keep up.

"Hey, Grandpa," I said,

"are we taking Curly to the park,

or is Curly taking us?"

Grandpa laughed.

"We go to the park every morning.

Curly knows the way."

Curly pulled us to a bench

in the middle of the park.

I watched kids swing higher and higher.

I wondered what I would see

from way up there.

Maybe I'd see a crime.

Maybe I'd see clues.

"Grandpa," I said, "I'm going on the swings."

"Sure," Grandpa said. "I'll get you started."

I took my big new magnifying glass

from my detective bag.

I put it in my pocket.

I sat on the swing seat.

I held on to the chains.

"Are you ready?" Grandpa asked.

"I'm ready," I said.

Grandpa pulled me back.

He gave me a big push.

Wow!

I was swinging high.

I looked down.

Grandpa and Curly looked small.

Everyone looked small.

I wondered what they would look like

through my big glass.

When I was really high,

I took out my magnifying glass.

No! Oh, no!

I was falling.

2. Detectives Find Things

I landed on the grass,

but I didn't cry.

Well, I did cry, but not a lot.

Grandpa ran to me.

"Are you hurt?" he asked.

"It's just my knees

and this hand that hurt," I said.

I showed Grandpa my hurting hand.

"You have no cuts," Grandpa said,

"and you're not bleeding. That's good.

Now you should sit and rest."

"I dropped my magnifying glass," I told Grandpa.

"I have to find it."

We looked in the bushes

near the swings.

We found a tennis ball,

a broken kite, a shoe, and half a golf club.

But we didn't find my magnifying glass.

"I need my detective bag," I said.

"I have detective things in there

that will help me find my glass."

I looked at all the benches.

"Grandpa," I asked,

"which bench is yours?"

"Oh, my," Grandpa said.

"There are so many benches.

I forget which one is mine."

"Don't worry," I said.

"I'm a detective. I'll find it."

My big magnifying glass was lost.

My detective bag was lost, too!

Detectives find things,

but I had lost things,

lots of things.

Right now I didn't feel

like a very good detective.

3. Clues Aren't Funny

I like to write clues on my detective pad,

but my detective pad was in my detective bag.

I would just have to remember them.

"Here's the first clue," I told Grandpa.

"Your bench is near the swings.

Here's the second clue.

There was a woman

with white hair sitting next to you."

Grandpa laughed.

"Clues aren't funny," I told him.

"Well," Grandpa said,

"I think your second clue is funny.

Look at the people in the park."

I looked.

Grandpa said,

"There are lots of women with white hair."

Grandpa was right.

"Well," I said,

"let's look near the swings."

There were lots of swings, too.

This sure was a big park.

"Hey," I said, and pointed.

"Look. There's your bench,

and there's my detective bag.

I do know how to find things.

I am a good detective."

"Oh, my!" Grandpa said.

"You found my bench,

and you found your detective bag,

but where's Curly?"

Curly was gone.

"Don't worry," I said.

"I'll find Curly.

I'm a detective,

and detectives find things."

4. Maybe He Was Stolen

Now I had two things to find,

my big, new magnifying glass and Curly.

I opened my detective bag.

I wondered what I could use to find Curly.

My detective pad would help.

I could write clues on it.

My small magnifying glass would help.

It would make small things bigger.

I didn't think I would need

my disguise hats, fakes noses, or beard.

I wasn't hiding from anyone.

And I didn't need my magnet,

green rope, or rubber gloves.

What I did need were clues.

I looked near the bench.

I found paw prints in the dirt.

I looked through my small glass

at the prints.

"Hey, Grandpa," I said,

"do these look like Curly's prints?"

"I'm sure they're his," Grandpa said,

"but they won't help you find Curly.

They end in the grass."

Detective work isn't easy.

I needed another clue.

"Hello," I said to the woman with white hair.

"Did you see a dog with curly hair?"

The woman looked up.

She smiled at me and at Grandpa.

She pointed to the ground

near Grandpa's side of the bench.

"He's sitting right there," she said.

Then the woman looked where she had pointed.

"Oh, my," she said. "That cute little dog is gone."

Grandpa said,

"Let's look for him."

The woman said, "I'll help.

My name is Sally."

Sally seemed nice,

but I didn't think she would be much help.

She was sitting right there

and hadn't even known that Curly ran off.

Grandpa, Sally, and I

walked everywhere in the park.

We even called out Curly's name.

"Curly! Curly! Curly!"

But we didn't find him.

We didn't know what to do,

so we went back to Grandpa's bench.

A good detective thinks of everything.

Right then I thought of something horrible.

Maybe Curly didn't run off.

Maybe he was stolen.

5. I've Got It!

"Did anyone come here and take Curly?"

I asked Sally.

"No," she told me.

"Are you sure?" Grandpa asked.

"Yes," she said.

"I was reading a newspaper.

If someone was here,

he would have blocked my light."

Sally and I sat on the bench.

Sally opened her newspaper,

and we pretended to read.

Grandpa walked to his side of the bench.

Sally was right.

Grandpa blocked our light.

I sat on the bench and thought.

A good detective asks lots of questions.

"When I was on the swings,"

I asked, "what was Curly doing?"

"He was sleeping," Grandpa said.

"Then you fell off the swings,

and I ran to you."

I thought about Curly.

A good detective thinks of everything.

Curly is smart, really smart.

He's a detective dog.

A detective dog thinks of everything, too.

I wondered what Curly thought

when he woke up and Grandpa was gone.

"I've got it!" I said.

"I know where to find Curly."

6. This Dog Likes Bones

"Where do you and Curly go,"

I asked Grandpa,

"when you leave the park?"

"We always go home," Grandpa said.

"Does Curly pull at his leash?"

"Sure he does," Grandpa said.

"He knows the way home."

"Then that's where he is," I said.

"Curly went home."

When Sally, Grandpa, and I
came close to Grandpa's house,
Curly ran to Grandpa.
"Would you like to come in,"
Grandpa asked me and Sally,

"for some milk or juice

and some cookies?"

"That would be nice," Sally said.

"Oh, no, it wouldn't," I said.

"We have to go back to the park

and find my magnifying glass."

Grandpa held onto Curly's leash

and Curly pulled him to the park.

Then I took Curly to the bushes near the swings.

I told him about the missing magnifying glass.

Curly is a smart detective dog.

He's also small enough

to look in places where

Grandpa and I were too big to look.

"Go, Curly," I said.

"Go find my magnifying glass."

Curly found a broken pencil and a mitten.

I put them in my detective bag.

I may need them one day

to solve a mystery.

Then Curly found my magnifying glass.

"Thank you. Thank you," I said.

I held out my arms, and Curly ran to me.

"Let's go home," Grandpa said

to Curly, Sally, and me.

"Let's get some milk, juice, and cookies."

Curly wagged his tail and barked.

"This dog likes Bones," I said.

"All dogs like bones," Sally said.

"Well," I told her.

"This dog likes this Bones.

This dog likes me,

Detective Jeffrey Bones."